ADVENTURES
OF A
CHRISTMAS
ELF

*More magical adventures
from Ben Miller:*

Diary of a Christmas Elf
Secrets of a Christmas Elf

The Night I Met Father Christmas
The Boy Who Made the World Disappear
The Day I Fell into A Fairytale
How I Became a Dog Called Midnight
The Night We Got Stuck in a Story
Once Upon a Legend

BEN MILLER

ADVENTURES
OF A
CHRISTMAS
ELF

Illustrated by
Christopher Naylor

SIMON & SCHUSTER

First published in Great Britain in 2023 by Simon & Schuster UK Ltd

1 3 5 7 9 10 8 6 4 2

Simon & Schuster UK Ltd
1st Floor, 222 Gray's Inn Road
London
WC1X 8HB

www.simonandschuster.co.uk

Simon & Schuster Australia, Sydney
Simon & Schuster India, New Delhi
A CIP catalogue record for this book is available from the British Library.

HB ISBN 978-1-3985-1584-0
Australian HB ISBN 978-1-3985-2363-0
eBook ISBN 978-1-3985-1586-4
Audio ISBN 978-1-3985-1585-7

Printed and bound by CPI Group (UK) Ltd, Croydon, CR0 4YY

For Lewis and Tony

Tuesday 27 October

I'm so lucky!

When I pulled back the curtain of my attic bedroom first thing this morning, I gasped in wonder. It had snowed in the night!

A bright crescent moon was smiling in the crisp dark sky, and all the rooftops in the East Village were gleaming white.

Quick as a flash, I rushed downstairs, pulled on my curly-toed boots, and burst out into the street. We live in the most crowded part of town, but there were no footprints or sleigh tracks anywhere. Everywhere I looked, the snow was completely untouched!

Dragging my foot, I wrote my name in the snow:

TOG WOZ ERE.

Then I stood still, looking up at the stars, breathing in the icy air . . .

As I skipped back inside to make breakfast for my younger brothers and sisters, I felt so grateful to be alive. Grateful to be a Christmas Elf, helping to make the toys for Father Christmas; grateful for my family, even though being the middle child of ten can be tricky at times; and grateful for my friend Holly, Father Christmas's daughter, because she always has my back, and together we've shared so many adventures.

But then, as I dusted the snowflakes from my cap, I remembered that underneath all that fresh snow, everything was still the same.

And my heart sank.

Because to be quite honest with you, things at the Workshop have been a little tense recently . . .

3

Wednesday 28 October

nother stressful day at work.

I need to explain. For two years running, some baddies have tried to steal Christmas, and everyone is worried that this year, they're going to try and do it again . . .

The first time, they tied Father Christmas up and

stole the sleigh with all the presents on it. Luckily, Holly and I managed to get it back, and Christmas was saved.

The second time, they kidnapped Father Christmas and held him to ransom! Luckily, Holly came to his rescue with the help of a robot Father Christmas she'd made.

Everyone's worried this year they'll try something even worse, so the Security Elves are on the lookout . . .

Thursday 29 October

Another tense day in the Workshop.

Christmas Place is so serious these days! We used to have so much fun, telling stories and cracking jokes while we worked. Even Steinar, the Right-Hand Elf, used to join in sometimes, playing his accordion for us to dance to whenever we met our targets.

Not any more. Everyone's so serious . . .

Holly even told me off for humming!

'Tog!' she hissed, looking up from her computer console. She's got really good at coding, and this year she's making video games. 'I'm trying to concentrate!'

'I can't help it!' I said. 'Every time I finish a cracker, I feel all warm and tingly inside.'

I looked at Ana, the new elf, for support, but she didn't look up from the skipping rope she was working on, the sort that lights up when you skip.

During hot chocolate break, I took Holly to one side and asked her if she was okay.

'Not really,' she said, her eyes filling with tears.

'You're worried about your dad, aren't you?' I asked.

Holly nodded. 'What if Ola and Eva try to kidnap him, like they did last year? Or worse?'

Ola and Eva are *seriously* bad baddies. Ola used to be Father Christmas's Left-Hand Elf, and Eva's a Luxembourgian billionaire who *hates* Christmas.

'If they do, they'll have me to deal with,' I said firmly, offering her my handkerchief. 'And Father Christmas's new Security Elves, of course.'

She cheered up a bit when I said that. Steinar has recruited a team of Security Elves to protect Father Christmas. Everywhere he goes, they go too, wearing mirrored sunglasses and talking to one another using microphones hidden in their sleeves. They've even

OLA | EVA | FINN | MAX

TOP SECRET
PROPERTY OF THE
SECURITY ELVES

taken the bells off their boots so no one can hear them coming.

'He mustn't go to the Halloween Party,' said Holly, gripping my arm.

'Why not?' I asked.

'Think about it,' said Holly. 'There'll be loads of people in costume, so it will be really easy for Ola, Eva, Max or Fizz to disguise themselves and sneak in. I'm convinced that's when they'll strike!'

Max and Fizz are Ola's son and daughter. They used to be Workshop Elves like Holly and me, which is why Holly feels like she can't trust anyone.

'Have you said anything?' I asked.

'Of course,' said Holly impatiently. 'But Dad won't listen. He said going to the party is vital for morale.'

I can see his point. The Halloween Party is a big fixture in the elf calendar, a time when everyone kicks back one last time before the Christmas rush, and we all love to see Father Christmas dressed up and skating like everyone else . . .

But I can see Holly's point too. It's a security risk.

I hope the party goes okay.

Friday 30 October

Disaster at the Workshop!

It all started when I decided to test my latest batch of Christmas crackers. I know not everyone has Christmas crackers, so I should probably explain what they are.

Basically, you pull them before you eat your Christmas dinner. You hold one end, the person next to you holds the other, and then you both pull. The crackers are made of paper, and when they come apart, they make a banging sound. One person usually wins, and they get all the things in the cracker: a paper hat, which you wear during dinner; a piece of paper with a joke on it; and a little toy. The other person gets nothing, which seems really unfair, but it adds massively to the excitement.

I needed to make sure my cracker snaps – that's the strip of cardboard inside the cracker that makes the noise – were working. So with a cracker in each hand, I offered the other ends to Ana and Holly.

'One, two, three . . .' I counted.

I was about to say 'pull', when the doors slammed open and two Security Elves rolled in like

12

commandos, barking instructions into their sleeve mics. Moments later, Father Christmas entered, surrounded by the rest of his Security Elves.

'Good morning, everyone!' he bellowed.

We all stood up, trying to catch a glimpse, but Father Christmas is rather short. His Security Elves, who are all quite large, were crowded around him,

and we couldn't quite see him over their heads.

'Ignore me, please,' boomed his familiar voice. 'I just want to observe. Pretend I'm not here.'

I took him at his word.

'Pull!' I said, and Holly, Ana and I pulled the crackers.

BANG! BANG!

The bangs sounded just like gunshots, and Father Christmas's Security Elves were on high alert. The largest of them pushed Father Christmas on to the ground, leaping on top of him, while the others flick-flacked across the Workshop floor, somersaulting from their hands to their feet like ninjas. Before I knew it, the Head Security Elf – a red-faced man with a moustache – had my arm halfway up my back, and was pressing my head against the workbench.

'Sorry!' I squeaked. 'We were testing crackers!'

The Head Security Elf picked up my half of the cracker from the workbench.

'What's this for?' he asked suspiciously, holding up a tiny plastic comb.

'Nothing, really,' I replied. 'It's one of five random gifts we put in all crackers.'

The Head Security Elf narrowed his eyes. 'And what are the other four?'

I counted them off on my hand.

'Cellophane fish that curls up when you put it on the palm of your hand, tiny pack of playing cards, tape measure, and a weird puzzle with two bits of twisted metal that no one has ever been able to undo.'

'What child,' began the Head Security Elf slowly, struggling to understand, 'asks for a tape measure for Christmas?'

But before I could answer, we were interrupted by the sound of moaning.

'I'm hit!' groaned Father Christmas, from down on the floor. 'My chest feels like it's under a heavy weight!'

'Sorry, Father Christmas,' said the large Security Elf who had jumped on top of him. 'That's me.'

He stood up, pulling Father Christmas to his feet.

'Oh,' said Father Christmas, checking himself over. 'Well, that's a relief. For a moment there, I thought I'd filled my last stocking.'

'Dad, you shouldn't be here!' hissed Holly anxiously. 'It's not safe!'

'I've got no choice, Holly,' replied Father

16

Christmas. 'Without me, this place would grind to a halt.'

'We can manage,' insisted Holly. 'I promise. Hide out somewhere – then come back to deliver the presents. If you don't, Christmas could be ruined forever!'

'Everything okay?' asked Steinar, the Right-Hand Elf, emerging from his office.

'Dad's on walkabout again,' said Holly.

'Torvil?' asked Steinar, peering over the top of his glasses. 'We talked about this.'

'Oh, bobbins and bed socks,' replied Father Christmas huffily. 'I'm not changing my routine just because a few baddies are on the prowl.'

'I'm sorry,' said Steinar firmly, 'but I must insist: essential appearances only. Everything else can be covered by Holly's robot.' He put a friendly hand on Father Christmas's shoulder. 'You need to take a step back.'

Father Christmas scowled, and didn't answer.

There was an awkward pause. Steinar looked meaningfully at the Head Security Elf.

'Let's get Big Dog back in the Kennel,' barked the Head Security Elf into his sleeve mic, and the remaining Security Elves shuffled back into position around Father Christmas, and moved back out.

'I'll take this,' said the Head Security Elf seriously, holding up my half of the Christmas cracker. 'For analysis.'

Saturday 31 October

It's Halloween!

Holly, Ana and I went down to the ice rink to help Bo and Bay, two of my older brothers and sisters, get it ready for the party.

The first bit, sweeping all the fresh snow off the ice, was quite hard work.

But the second part, decorating, was so much fun!

We draped fake spider webs between the lanterns, then hung up some giant rubber spiders for extra effect. It looked so creepy!

No sooner had we finished than who should come charging over the brow of the neighbouring hill but Father Christmas, waving and shouting on his sleigh!

To begin with, of course, we were all delighted. Father Christmas always makes a few test-runs before the big day, and it's considered very lucky if you see him. But then, as we watched him approach, our joy turned to confusion.

'That's weird,' I said to Holly. 'Usually the reindeer are at the front. But look – they're all at the back.'

Holly's eyes widened.

'The reins!' she exclaimed. 'They've snapped! He's waving and shouting because he's in trouble!'

It was true!

The sleigh was out of control, and Father Christmas was rushing down the hillside towards us at breakneck speed, the reindeer chasing along behind, trying to keep up!

'Help!' howled Father Christmas.

Out of the corner of my eye, I glimpsed the huge pile of snow we had swept, and suddenly I knew what to do.

'Go that way!' I shouted to Rudolph. 'Aim for the snow!'

Hearing my words, my old friend put on a surge

of speed and nudged the front of the sleigh with his nose, steering it towards the pile of snow!

The next thing we knew, the sleigh came hurtling across the ice, straight into the white fluffy mound!

Rudolph and the other reindeer skidded to a halt, and for a moment, there was silence.

Then we all rushed forward, pushing back the snow to reveal Father Christmas, coughing and spluttering.

'What happened?' asked Holly.

'I have no idea!' said Father Christmas, through a mouthful of snow. 'The reins came away in my hands.'

'Lucky it happened on the ground,' added Rudolph breathlessly. 'If we'd been up in the air, it could have been really serious.'

'Sabotage!' exclaimed Holly.

'Now, now,' said Father Christmas, raising his hands in a calming gesture. 'Let's not jump to conclusions.'

'Dad,' said Holly. 'Please tell me this means you're not coming to the party tonight?'

'Those reins are nearly five hundred years old,' said Father Christmas patiently. 'They were bound to break some time.'

'This wasn't an accident!' shrieked Holly. 'Why can't you see that? This was Ola and Eva – I know it was.'

'If I'm not here tonight to raise everyone's spirits,' insisted Father Christmas, 'we won't complete all the toys before Christmas. Besides . . .' A twinkle appeared in his eye. 'I've chosen a killer outfit.'

Sunday 1 November

Last night, my worst fears came true.

The Halloween Party on the ice rink is usually one of my favourite times of the whole year, but last night, I was so sick with worry, I couldn't enjoy it at all.

As I got dressed into my tarantula costume, my mind was working overtime.

Father Christmas would have his Security Elves with him, of course, but what use would they be if the baddies came in disguise?

I got there early and picked up my skates from Bo and Bay's hut – they always put some skates aside for me.

'Help yourself,' said Bo when I arrived. 'All the skates are over there, with everyone's names on.'

Sure enough, there they were: a really nice black pair, perfect for my outfit. While I was lacing them up, I noticed a pink pair with white fur lining and sparkles. They had Father Christmas's name on, which made me wonder what his costume was going to be . . .

Feeling anxious, I wandered out on to the ice. It was empty and bathed in an eerie low mist, so that the cobwebs, spiders and orange lanterns looked scarier than ever.

I felt a hand on my shoulder – and jumped!

'Tog!'

It was Holly, dressed as a headless horsewoman. The outfit was very effective, and it took me a moment to spot her eyes, which I eventually realised were in her chest!

'You're here early,' she said. 'Are you thinking what I'm thinking?'

I nodded. 'We need to keep a close eye on your dad.'

'And everyone else,' said Holly. 'Ola, Max, Fizz or Eva might come in disguise like they did last year. Or . . .'

It was Holly, dressed as a headless horsewoman

I leaned in closer.

'There may be a traitor in our midst,' she whispered.

'Like who?' I asked.

Holly glanced over her shoulder, making sure she was alone.

'What about Ana?' she said quietly.

I frowned. 'Really?'

'Think about it. Max was a Workshop Elf. Fizz was a Workshop Elf. Ana – ' she lowered her voice to a whisper – 'is also Workshop Elf.'

I raised my eyebrows. 'But she's so quiet.'

'Too quiet,' said Holly knowingly.

'Tog!' came a chorus of voices, interrupting us, and I turned to see my younger siblings Twig, Leaf, Plum and Pin skating towards us. Twig was a witch with a broom, Leaf was a ghost, Plum was a pumpkin, and Pin was a bat.

They looked amazing!

We admired one another's outfits as a flood of people arrived. Bo powered up his DJ decks, pumping out Halloween tunes, and everyone started to dance.

Holly and I scoured the crowd, checking for anything suspicious . . .

Suddenly I spotted a knight in full medieval armour. My mind flashed back to Eva's castle in Luxembourg; hadn't I seen something similar there, standing in a hallway as decoration?

'Who's that?' I asked Holly.

Holly shrugged.

'Steinar!' I called. 'Is that you?'

The knight gave us the thumbs-up.

We were about to investigate further, when a

loud cheer went up: Father Christmas had arrived, dressed as a Fairy Godmother, sitting in an open gold carriage, pulled by his Security Elves, who were all dressed as white mice!

Holly and I looked at one another nervously.

The crowd around him began to go crazy, clapping and cheering!

Enjoying the attention, Father Christmas stepped down from the carriage, helped by the Head Security Elf. Then, while everyone flocked around, Father Christmas laced up his furry pink boots, and skated out on to the ice!

The crowd went wild!

Which was when I noticed something odd . . .

It was hard to be sure because of the mist, but . . .

Father's Christmas's skates were steaming!

As I watched, Father Christmas raised his wand

and began to pirouette, turning faster and faster.

There was the sound of ice cracking, and I dived forward just in time to grab Father Christmas's hands, a split second before his skates melted a hole in the ice, and he plunged down into the icy water!

I've tried to remember exactly what happened next, but to be quite honest, it's a bit of a blur. Lots of other people rushed forward to help, I remember that much, and we dragged Father Christmas to safety. He was soaked to the skin, so we bundled him into the hut and helped him out of his wet ballerina dress. Holly found a hot-water bottle and pressed it to his chest before wrapping him up in a warm blanket.

'My feet!' chattered Father Christmas. 'They're freezing!'

As quickly as I could, I unlaced his skates, emptying

There was the sound of ice cracking

them of water. Which was when I noticed something a little bit out of the ordinary.

'Holly!' I hissed. 'The blades are still warm!'

Eyeing me warily, Holly removed a mitten and touched the blade of the skate. Her eyes widened, and she pulled her hand back in alarm.

'Dad, your skates!' she blurted. 'Someone heated them up! Feel!'

Frowning, Father Christmas stretched out his hand. His fingers touched the metal, and his expression turned from puzzlement to shock.

'B-but . . . who could have done that?' he stuttered.

'I told you,' said Holly. 'Ola and Eva are out to get you. The North Pole is not safe.'

Monday 2 November

The mood at work today was very sombre. There was no singing and dancing, and during hot chocolate break, everyone sipped in silence.

We were all still in shock at the attempt on Father Christmas's life.

Holly, Ana and I hardly spoke; we just worked on

our toys. I tried to make up jokes for the crackers, but I wasn't in the mood.

Then, as I was about to leave, Holly took me to one side.

'Thank you,' she said. 'For always having Dad's back.'

'That's okay,' I replied.

I sensed there was more, so I waited.

'There's a family meeting,' she said. 'Tonight. At Christmas Lodge. I'd really like you to come.'

I love my visits to Christmas Lodge, the reindeer ranch in the Arctic Hills where Father Christmas and his family live, and even though the circumstances were less than ideal, I still felt a twinge of excitement at the thought of being in that magical place once again. As Holly and I raced through the town, pulled by a team of huskies, I felt a surge of Christmas spirit. Somehow, I told myself, we would get through these dark times, and emerge stronger than ever!

Soon we were plunging down into the forest, the dogs weaving right and left as the path wound its way among the snow-caked fir trees, then climbing again, until we found ourselves cresting a rise, the twinkling lights of Christmas Lodge just visible at the foot of the Arctic Hills.

'Yah!' called Holly again, urging the dogs on. The sled picked up speed, and – as if the whole scene didn't look festive enough – it began to snow again, giant snowflakes hanging in the air like paper lanterns. The moment was so perfect, I closed my eyes, hoping to save a snapshot. When I opened them again, we were racing up the drive, just yards from the house.

'Woah!' called Holly, pulling on the reins, and the sled skidded to a halt.

'Tog!' called Mrs Christmas, throwing open the front door, welcoming me into the glow. 'Come inside while Holly sees to the dogs.'

I gave Mrs Christmas a giant hug, then followed her into the warmth of the house.

The scene that greeted me was as Christmassy as it gets. There were roaring fires in every room, their mantelpieces groaning with holly, ivy and mistletoe, and I lost count of the number of Christmas trees I saw, each one dripping with decorations, and surrounded by a landslide of lovingly wrapped presents.

And the scent!

Why do certain houses smell so different, as if

they are wearing their very own brand of perfume?

I took a deep breath, my nose painting delicious pictures of cinnamon sticks, satsuma peel and fresh brown paper . . .

But there was no time to waste.

'This way,' said Mrs Christmas, leading me through to a large oak-beamed room. 'The meeting's just started.'

As I entered, Steinar, the Right-Hand Elf, was in full flow; sitting beside him, still shivering with cold, was Father Christmas; next to him was the Head Security Elf; and dotted around the room, listening attentively, were Holly's nine older brothers and sisters.

'Glad you could join us, Tog,' said Steinar. 'Following a thorough investigation, it's clear that Halloween night's incident was no accident.'

A handkerchief fluttered out of Father Christmas's pocket, and he let rip an enormous sneeze.

'Bless you,' said Steinar with a brief smile. Then his expression darkened. 'Someone heated up Father Christmas's skates before he put them on. The question is: who?'

'May I?' offered the Head Security Elf, raising his hand.

'Go ahead,' said Steinar self-importantly.

'It could have been anyone at the party. And whoever heated up the skates probably tampered with the reins too – hence the unfortunate event earlier the same day, when Father Christmas found himself in charge of an out-of-control sleigh.'

Holly gave me an *I told you* so look.

'An earlier event, when some cracker snaps were detonated in the Workshop, proved to be a red herring,' added the Head Security Elf, looking me straight in the eye.

'All of which leads me to suggest,' said Steinar gravely, 'that we take drastic measures.'

There was a pause.

'What sort of measures?' asked Father Christmas.

'Torvil,' said Steinar, using Father Christmas's first name, which hardly anyone ever did. 'I think it's time you took a holiday.'

Tuesday 3 November

No time to write! I've got to pack because . . .

Drum roll . . .

I'm going to the Maldives!

Wednesday 4 November

I'm having to pinch myself to believe this is real!

I'm sitting in seat 56A on a jumbo jet.

It's right next to the toilets, which is really handy because I have been feeling a tiny bit airsick.

And guess who's in seat 56B?

That's right: Father Christmas!

It's the middle of the night, and he's fast asleep, so

I'm trying to write quietly so I don't wake him . . .

I've been chosen to go with him to the Maldives!

If you don't know what the Maldives are — and to be quite honest, before Steinar gave me this assignment, I didn't — let me tell you now: they are a tiny group of islands in the Indian Ocean, about 750 kilometres from the southern tip of India.

The plan is for Father Christmas and me to lie low while Holly and Steinar try to catch the baddies.

I'm delighted because, like most elves, I've never had a holiday!

Father Christmas isn't happy about it at all though. When Steinar suggested he use this as an opportunity to rest and recharge, he said he'd never taken any time off in five hundred years, and wasn't going to start now. He's brought all his maps so he can prepare his route, and a copy of the Naughty and

Nice Lists so that he can read up on all the kids. He's even brought his sack full of letters, which he says he's going to answer in his room while I hang out on the beach.

That's all for now. I'll tell you more when we get there.

Thursday 5 November

I'm in the Maldives!

My room is amazing!

The view couldn't be more different to the one from my bedroom in the East Village! There, I can see crowded rooftops, drenched in snow, backed by the Arctic Hills. Here, all I can see is sand, crystal-clear turquoise water and bright blue sky.

I don't think I've ever been anywhere more relaxing.

There's even a bath in the window, so you can have a soak while you gaze at the Indian Ocean . . .

It was quite a long journey. First, we flew from the North Pole to Malé, the main island. Then we caught a tiny seaplane, and landed on the ocean next to our island.

The people that work here are so friendly, and they were all waiting on the jetty to meet us, dressed in white. They offered us each a glass of passion fruit juice with a pretty flower in.

Father Christmas was still in quite a bad mood, and he said he didn't want his, so I had two!

There's a beautiful sunset, so I'm going to watch the sun go down, then plunge into my comfy-looking bed . . .

Friday 6 November

Two words:

Breakfast Buffet.

I've never seen anything like it! Pancakes, pastries, waffles, maple syrup, bacon and tropical fruits, all laid out on white-linen-covered tables!

And I had it all to myself!

Well, nearly. There's a man and a lady here, on

honeymoon, from Atlanta in America. He's a rapper called In-Cent, and she's a music producer called Leontine. They're very nice, but I got the impression they'd like to be left alone, so I sat on my own at a table on the other side of the room.

I waited all morning for Father Christmas to come down, but he never appeared, so in the end, I put some nice bits and pieces on a plate and took it up to his room.

There was a DO NOT DISTURB sign on his door, and it took ages for him to answer.

The room was very cold, and he was wearing the same woolly sweater he had worn during the flight. I could see that his desk light was on, and there was a pile of children's letters on his desk. Even working at elf

speed, it was going to take him days to get through them . . .

'Yes?' he asked gruffly.

'I brought you some breakfast,' I said hopefully. 'And I wondered if afterwards, you'd like to come for a swim?'

He fixed me with his bright blue eyes. 'Have you any idea,' he asked, 'how much work I have to do at Christmas?'

I said I didn't.

'And how much harder it is to get it done in this infernal place?'

I said I didn't know that either.

'This might be a holiday for you, Tog,' he said sternly. 'But for me, there's no such thing.'

He paused in the doorway.

'One last thing,' he said. 'Can you tell me what this says?'

He pointed to the sign on the door handle.

'*Do Not Disturb*,' I said.

'Good,' said Father Christmas. 'I was beginning to wonder.'

Then he closed the door.

Saturday 7 November

I had an amazing day on the beach!

The Do Not Disturb sign was still on Father Christmas's door, so I borrowed some equipment from a nice Australian man called Darren at the dive school and went snorkelling.

When I put my head under the water, I saw

hundreds of coloured fish! There were green fish, pink fish, red fish and yellowy-orange fish; fish with spikes, spots, stripes and blotches.

I decided to pretend I was a shark, and swam after them . . .

I was so busy chasing them, I didn't spot the honeymoon couple were in the water too. When I came up for air, they were kissing right beside me!

'Morning!' I said brightly, then ducked back under.

I felt so embarrassed.

It was all so beautiful below the surface that I soon got over it.

One thing was quite scary though. If you swim out past the sand, to where the coral is, the ocean floor suddenly drops away beneath you like a cliff . . .

When I was handing the equipment back, Darren told me the Maldives are volcanic, and each island is really a tall, thin column in the Indian Ocean, with just the top poking out of the water.

How amazing is that?

It did make me think, though, that while we might be safe here on the island, there's danger lurking all around . . .

Which reminds me: I must check in with Holly and see how things are going back at the North Pole.

Sunday 8 November

First thing after breakfast – which, as usual, was utterly fantastic – I called Holly to check in.

'How's Dad?' she asked. 'I'm really missing him.'

'Okay, I think,' I replied. 'He's having breakfast in his room again, while he finalises his delivery route.'

Holly sighed.

'That's such a shame,' she said. 'Who goes to the Maldives and stays in their room?'

'Maybe he'll come snorkelling tomorrow,' I said hopefully. 'The fish are incredible. And how about you? Have you caught the baddies?'

'Not yet,' she replied. 'No one's noticed Dad's missing, though, which is good. They all think the robot is him.'

'So what's the plan?' I asked.

'It's Toy Testing Day next week,' said Holly. 'When Dad's supposed to check out the toys. Everyone from the village is invited, so the baddies are bound to try something. And when they do, we'll be ready for them!'

Monday 9 November

Went snorkelling again.

It was really fun.

Father Christmas is still in his room, working. At least, that's my best guess, because the Do Not Disturb sign is still on his door.

I saw the honeymoon couple at lunchtime, at the

beach restaurant, but when they saw me coming, they got up to leave.

Checked in with Holly, but no news.

Tuesday 10 November

Went snorkelling again.

Wednesday 11 November

S tarting to feel a teensy bit lonely.

After breakfast, I saw Leontine and In-Cent on the beach. In-Cent was putting sunscreen on Leontine's back, which was very sensible, because the sun here is very bright. I don't think they heard me coming, though, because when I said hello,

In-Cent gave a little shout and dropped the bottle of sunscreen in the sand.

I always forget: humans have a hard time hearing elves. Which is why Father Christmas is able to deliver his presents without waking the children up.

I think they enjoyed chatting to me, because they kept looking at one another and smiling. Although when I went to fetch a towel so I could sit next to them, they'd gone . . .

Thursday 12 November

More snorkelling.
Still no sign of Father Christmas.

Friday 13 November

I'M SO BORED.

Saturday 14 November

I HATE THE MALDIVES.

Sunday 15 November

J ust got off the phone to Holly. I can't believe what she told me!

It was Toy Testing Day today . . .

Everyone was crowded into the Workshop, and Father Christmas was going down the line, chatting to all the Workshop Elves and checking all the different toys.

Except, of course, it wasn't really Father Christmas; it was the robot.

Everything went smoothly, until the very last toy in the line – a cuddly teddy bear.

'Hello, there,' said Robot Father Christmas to the elf who'd made it. 'And what might your name be?'

'Pippin,' said the elf.

'Have you been good?' asked Robot Father Christmas.

Pippin looked a little confused, as if that hadn't been the question he was expecting. Robot Father Christmas was built to talk to children in the grotto, so sometimes the things he says are a little bit odd.

'Err . . . yes,' said Pippin. 'At least, I hope so. I've been making these,' he added, handing over the teddy.

Robot Father Christmas gave the bear a cuddle.

'What would you like for Christmas?' he asked Pippin.

'Err . . . to not start work straight away on the toys for next year?' suggested Pippin hopefully.

Which was when Holly noticed the bear was ticking!

'Duck!' she yelled.

But it was too late! There was a deafening bang, and when the smoke cleared, everyone gasped.

Robot Father Christmas's head had been blown clean off!

'Don't forget to leave me a mince pie and a drink,' said the robot's head cheerfully, from down on the floor. 'And a carrot for the reindeer!'

Tuesday 17 November

Missed a day of my diary.

I was so stressed out about the exploding teddy bear blowing the robot's head off, I had to spend twenty-four hours in a darkened room.

The robot can easily be repaired, but imagine

if that had actually been Father Christmas! This sabotage is getting really dangerous.

Anyway, back to my conversation with Holly.

'Did you notice anything unusual at all?' I asked. 'That might help us work out who was behind it?'

There was a pause, while Holly wracked her brains.

'There was something . . .' she said hesitatingly.

'What?'

'Just before the bang, on the other side of the toy table, I thought I saw the knight in armour.'

'The one from the Halloween Party?' I gasped

'Exactly,' said Holly. 'But by the time the smoke had cleared, he was gone.'

'Steinar!' I gasped. 'I can't believe he'd do this!

Father Christmas will be devastated . . .'

'Wait,' said Holly, her mind clearly working overtime. 'We don't *know* that it was Steinar in that outfit. Just because he waved when we called out to him, doesn't mean it was him. It could have been anyone. Like Ana, for instance.'

'Oh don't start on her again!' I replied.

'Well, she wasn't at Toy Testing Day.'

'Where was she?' I asked.

'She called in sick.'

I thought for a moment. 'And where was Steinar?' I asked in my best detective voice.

'He wasn't there either,' replied Holly. 'A delivery had just arrived, so he popped out to sign for it.'

'Right,' I replied, catching up. 'So it could be

70

either of them. Or come to think of it, anyone.'

'Yup,' said Holly. 'And what's worse – the traitor knows Robot Father Christmas isn't the real one now, so they won't bother trying again.'

I gulped.

'Well, then,' I told her. 'You'd better find out who was in that suit of armour.'

Wednesday 18 November

Father Christmas has finally left his room!

I think it was the shock of what happened on Toy Testing Day.

I wasn't sure whether to tell him, because of the Do Not Disturb sign, but in the end I decided he had to know, and I knocked and knocked until he answered.

He was cross at first, but then, as I described the robot's head being blown off, he went quiet.

'Hmm,' he said, stroking his long white beard.

'Are you okay?' I asked.

'You and I need to talk this through,' he said thoughtfully. 'What's this I hear . . .' he began. 'About a breakfast buffet?'

When I led him into the dining room, he couldn't believe it!

'Is that really a chocolate fountain?' he asked. 'And is that carrot cake? I *adore* carrot cake!'

We filled our plates, and walked out on to the terrace, the sunshine dancing on the clear blue water.

Father Christmas made me tell him the whole story of the Toy Testing Day all over again, and this time I told him about the knight in armour, and how

73

Holly and I were trying to find out who had been wearing it.

'I did wonder,' he said, dabbing his mouth with a linen napkin, 'whether all this hiding-away-at-a-secret-location stuff was really necessary. But exploding teddy bears . . .' He stared out to sea wistfully. 'That's serious. Ola and Eva are more desperate than we thought.'

I said I agreed.

'I guess I really am stuck here,' said Father Christmas. 'Until Holly finds out who was in that suit of armour.'

I agreed with that too.

There was a pause, while Father Christmas stared at the sea a bit more.

'I've answered all the children's letters,' he mused. 'I've finalised the Nice List, and I've looked up everyone's house on my special map. What do you say —' he fixed me with his bright blue eyes — 'to hitting the beach?'

Thursday 19 November

After all the tension of the last few days, it was great to see Father Christmas unwind.

I took him all around the island, and we went paddling in the lagoon. I think he really enjoyed himself.

I have to admit, at times I had to pinch myself — me, Tog Harket, a poor elf from the East Village, hanging out with Father Christmas!

He told me some great stories about things that have happened when he's been delivering presents.

Once, he was climbing back up the chimney, when a dog jumped up and bit his bottom! He had to stuff his hat in his mouth to stop himself from shouting and waking everyone up!

It's great to see him relax a bit, given all the stress he's been under.

Friday 20 November

Father Christmas was waiting for me at breakfast, wearing a Hawaiian shirt, swimming shorts, flip-flops and shades.

'Look what I found!' he exclaimed, showing me a tiny

bar of chocolate. 'When I got back to my room last night, someone had turned down the sheets and put this on my pillow!'

'They do that every night,' I said. 'You must have taken down your *Do Not Disturb* sign.'

'A little chocolate,' he said, misty-eyed. 'I mean, how thoughtful!'

He went silent, turning the chocolate over in his hands.

'I could really get used to it here,' he said. 'Maybe I'll come back one day, with the family, when these awful baddies are safely behind bars.'

As we were leaving, I introduced Father Christmas to In-Cent and Leontine. 'Hi, guys,' I said. 'This is Father Chris—'

Then I stopped, because I realised I'd nearly blown Father Christmas's cover!

'My father, Chris,' I said quickly.

Father Christmas shook their hands.

'Did we meet before, Chris?' asked In-Cent. 'You seem kind of familiar . . .'

'I've just got one of those faces,' said Father Christmas.

Saturday 21 November

Still no news from Holly, so I took Father Christmas to check out the dive school. Darren suggested a ride on the banana boat.

'Can I ask how old you are, Chris?' asked Darren, as he filled in the risk-assessment form.

'Five hundred and seventy-three,' said Father Christmas.

Darren looked up and frowned.

'I mean, seventy-three,' said Father Christmas quickly.

A banana boat, I discovered, is a big inflatable banana with seats on. Father Christmas sat in front, and I went behind. Darren pulled us along with the motorboat, and after we'd gone up and down the

beach a few times, he took us out into deep water and started making really sharp turns!

We managed to stay on for the first two turns, but the third one sent us flying!

I laughed so much, I swallowed some seawater and had to come back to my room for a lie-down.

Sunday 22 November

No news, so Father Christmas and I went paddleboarding!

You absolutely have to try it – it's amazing.

A paddleboard is like a giant surfboard, but instead of catching waves, you stand on it and use a paddle to cruise along the top of the water!

We went all the way around the island, and when we got to the lagoon, I saw a giant turtle, swimming just below us!

Father Christmas said it was one of the most magical things he'd ever experienced, and I had to agree with him.

I wonder what we'll try next?

Monday 23 November

Kayaking!
Catamaraning!
Scuba-diving!

Tuesday 24 November

When I got back to my room after breakfast, guess who I saw a missed call from?

Holly!

'Please let this be good news,' I said to myself, and called her back.

It was!

'We caught the baddy!' she said breathlessly.

I gave a little shout of joy!

'It was Nutmeg, the stable-boy!'

I frowned. Nutmeg was one of the kindest elves I knew! Had mucking out the reindeer turned him against Father Christmas? I'd done that job myself once, and I'd had to burn my dungarees afterwards because the smell just wouldn't go away . . .

'We caught him red-handed,' she continued. 'Not only did we find the gunpowder used to make the exploding cuddly toy, but we also found the helmet from the coat of arms, hidden behind the bag of magic oats.'

'Oh wow!' I said. 'So it's safe to come home?'

'Tog?' asked Holly. 'Are you out of your mind?'

'Maybe?' I said cautiously.

88

'Nutmeg was just the front elf. Eva, Ola, Max, and Fizz are all still at large! I was talking to Ana about it, just now. If Dad comes out of hiding, he's toast!'

I went a bit quiet at that point, because I was confused.

The last I knew, Holly was sure that Ana was one of Ola and Eva's spies!

'The safest thing,' said Holly, 'is for you to stay put, out of harm's way, and be back for Christmas Eve.'

When I went to tell Father Christmas, he went very quiet.

'No offence, Tog,' he said. 'I've enjoyed our time together. But I can't stay here. Not when everyone I love is at the North Pole.'

'I know,' I said. 'It's a horrible choice to make, Christmas or your family. But imagine if something happened to you. The children of the world would have no presents . . .'

Father Christmas nodded silently.

'Here,' I said. 'Something to cheer you up.'

Father Christmas looked at the computer cartridge I had given him.

'It's called *Ski Quest*,' I said.

'I'm not really into video games,' said Father Christmas uncertainly. 'I'm more of a doer than a gamer, if you know what I mean.'

'It's the one Holly's been working on,' I said. 'I thought you might like to take a look.'

'Ah!' said Father Christmas, his eyes lighting up. 'In that case . . .'

Wednesday 25 November

No sign of Father Christmas today, so I went to see if he was in his room. I'm pretty sure he was in – I could hear the sound of a motorboat coming from the TV – but I don't think he heard me knocking.

I guess he wants a bit of alone time.

Checked in with Holly, but I caught her at a bad time, because she was going skating with Ana.

'I tell her everything!' breezed Holly. 'She's my best friend.'

I felt a twinge in my stomach when she said that. I must have had one too many pastries at the breakfast buffet this morning.

Holly must have sensed my discomfort, because she said quickly, 'One of them, anyway. You're going to love her!'

Thursday 26 November

Father Christmas stayed in his room, so I read a coffee-table book about trees.

Friday 27 November

Read another coffee-table book about trees.

Saturday 28 November

Read a third coffee-table book about trees.

Sunday 29 November

Really worried about Father Christmas, so I ended up asking one of the housekeeping staff to let me into his room. And here's a really strange coincidence: as he opened the door, I saw he had candy canes tattooed on his wrist, just like Ola!

So glad I did!

Island Quest was playing on the TV.

There were empty bags of popcorn everywhere, and he was lying on the bed, snoring, holding a game controller. There were dark circles around his eyes, and the bits around his beard badly needed a trim.

'Father Christmas!' I said. 'Wake up!'

He jolted upright.

'Where am I?' he asked, blinking in confusion.

'In your room,' I said. 'You've been playing *Island Quest* non-stop for nearly a week!'

'No I haven't,' said Father Christmas defiantly.

'The controller is in your hand!' I exclaimed. 'And look – the runtime is one hundred and six hours.'

'I may have played a couple of games,' said Father Christmas defensively.

I decided to let it go.

'Why don't you go and see Darren?' I asked. 'He can take you waterskiing for real!'

'Don't be silly,' said Father Christmas, patting his tummy. 'He'll never find a wetsuit to fit me.'

'Darren's a big guy,' I replied. 'If he can find a wetsuit, anyone can.'

When I closed the door, the man from housekeeping was still there with his trolley, as if he had been listening to our conversation. I flashed him a warm smile, and he went back to work.

That's how lovely the staff are here. Every single one of them takes an interest in the well-being of their guests.

Monday 30 November

Today was a huge, huge disaster.

I don't know where to begin . . .

Father Christmas wasn't at breakfast, and I began to worry just a tiny bit that something might have happened to him.

But I shrugged it off.

I mean, no-one knew we were here, apart from his family. And the Security Elves, of course, but they were a watertight operation.

He wasn't in his room either, or the lobby.

I ran all up and down the hotel, but I couldn't find him anywhere.

I was beginning to panic when I spotted In-Cent and Leontine on the beach, staring out to sea, shaking their heads in disbelief.

Then I saw what they were looking at.

Father Christmas was bobbing along the horizon, waterskiing!

'Yo Daddy got some serious moves,' said In-Cent, nodding his head appreciatively.

'Got those skis on lock,' added Leontine.

Father Christmas had obviously learned lots of skills playing *Island Quest*, because he was really showing off, skiing with one foot in the handle of the rope, skiing backwards, and even doing a flip in the air!

Darren made a turn with the boat, and Father Christmas swooshed past him, throwing up a wall of spray. In-Cent, Leontine, and I all cheered!

Which was when Darren's wig blew off!

At first, I laughed. Then I frowned in confusion.

That wasn't Darren at the helm . . .

It was Ola!

My mind flashed back to the candy canes on the wrist of man from housekeeping . . .

A wave of alarm crashed over me . . .

Our cover had been blown!

Too late, I realised Ola was lining Father Christmas up for an enormous jump!

'No!' I yelled, waving my hands up and down. 'Bail! Bail!'

But as Ola shot past the ramp, Father Christmas saw me waving, and lost concentration!

The next thing I knew, Father Christmas hit the ramp and shot high in the air, somersaulting over and over, arms and legs and skis flailing, before wiping out hard in a colossal splash!

Then he vanished!

All we could see were his waterskis bobbing on the surface.

I felt my blood run cold.

A low-flying helicopter swept across the water, with Eva, Max, and Fizz in the cockpit!

Max and Finn threw a rope for Ola, winching him up!

'Help!' I yelled, rushing into the water. 'Help!'

I plunged into the water, closely followed by In-Cent and Leontine, and the three of us swam as fast as we could to the spot where we had last seen Father Christmas.

'Father Christmas!' I called. 'Father Christmas!' But the noise from the chopper was so loud I couldn't hear my own voice.

I tried diving under the surface, but without my facemask, I couldn't see a thing.

In-Cent and Leontine tried diving too.

But it was useless.

Ola was now back in the helicopter, high-fiving Eva, Max, and Fizz. Eva worked the controls, and the four of them sped off noisily, vanishing over the horizon.

I felt like there was a brick in my stomach.

The baddies had done it. Father Christmas was gone for good.

Then suddenly Father Christmas burst to the surface, coughing and spluttering!

In-Cent, Leontine, and I shouted for joy!

Working together, we hauled him aboard the motorboat, and sped to the shore.

In-Cent and I helped Father Christmas up the beach, sitting him down on a sun lounger. He seemed a little out of sorts, so I checked him over, making sure no bones were broken. It was then that I noticed the bruise on his temple . . .

'Ho ho ho,' he said to Leontine in a cheery voice. 'Hello there. And what might your name be?'

'Leontine,' replied In-Cent's bride awkwardly. 'We already met.'

'Have you been good?' asked Father Christmas.

'Excuse me?' asked Leontine, glancing at In-Cent.

'What would you like for Christmas?' Father Christmas beamed, patting his lap as if he expected Leontine to sit on it.

'That's enough, Chris,' said In-Cent, stepping forward.

I jumped in quickly to diffuse the situation.

'In-Cent,' I said gravely. 'We need to get Father Christmas – I mean Chris – I mean Dad – to a hospital.'

Tuesday 1 December

I'm at the hospital in Malé, the main island of the Maldives.

Darren drove us here in the motorboat.

Oh, I forgot to tell you – we found him tied up in his hut!

Someone bashed him over the head, and when he woke up he had ropes around him.

It must have been Ola.

An ambulance met us at the harbour and drove us straight here. They even put the siren on!

I glimpsed a little bit of the city as we drove. It's very different to the island where the hotel is. We drove through an area that reminded me of the East Village, back at the North Pole, where I grew up. There were lots of houses packed together, and I saw people sleeping in doorways. I guess not everywhere in the Maldives looks like our hotel . . .

When we arrived at the hospital, they rushed Father Christmas straight into Emergency.

I've been waiting here ever since.

I hope he's okay.

Wednesday 2 December

F inally got to see Father Christmas. When I
got to the ward, he was sitting up in bed,
back to his old self.

I felt a wave of relief.

'Tog!' he said. 'Where have you been?'

I told him all about Ola disguising himself as
Darren.

'Disgraceful,' he said shaking his head in disbelief. 'The depths that man will sink to.'

'The question is,' I said, 'how did he know we were here?'

Father Christmas sighed.

'Nutmeg?' he asked.

I shook my head. 'Nutmeg thought the robot was you, remember? It has to be someone else.'

Father Christmas shrugged.

'We need to get back,' he said. 'There's work to be done.'

'I know,' I said gently. 'They want to keep you in for a bit, to make sure you've made a full recovery. But I'm sure we can go soon.'

'Ridiculous! I'm fine,' said Father Christmas, climbing out of bed and pulling on his cargo shorts. 'Send them in!'

'Excuse me, sir!' said an important-looking doctor, entering with a group of medical students. I could see from her badge her name was Dr Kadija Beefan. 'I said to stay in bed.'

'Listen,' said Father Christmas, lowering his voice, and beckoning Dr Beefan towards him. 'Between you and me, you may not realise this, but I am actually Father Christmas, and if I don't get back to the North Pole soon, there are going to be a lot of very disappointed little girls and boys who don't get their presents this year . . .'

'Ohhhhh-kay!' said the doctor, throwing her students a worried look. 'First, I think we'd better send you for a few more tests.'

'Nonsense!' said Father Christmas. 'I'm fit as a

fiddle! Come on, Tog . . . we're leaving.'

'Not right now, you're not, sir,' said Doctor Beefan firmly.

There was a bit of a struggle, and Doctor Beefan called for assistance. The next thing I knew, Father Christmas was being strapped into a chair and wheeled away.

'Tog!' he shouted. 'Get me out of here!'

PRESCRIPTION

Patient Name: _____

Address _____

Thursday 3 December

They've put Father Christmas in a special ward at the hospital! I can't even visit him! I asked Doctor Beefan when he'd be coming out, and she just shrugged and said, 'That's a very difficult question to answer.'

Basically, she doesn't believe he's Father Christmas. She thinks his bang on the head has sent him crazy!

Even worse, I slept on the chairs in reception, and when I woke up, someone had stolen my phone and all my money.

So I can't even call Holly to tell her what's happened.

My diary's been stolen too! All I could find in the wastepaper basket was this measly scrap of paper!

get well soon!

Thursday 10 December

Still at the hospital. What are we going to do? We need to get back for Christmas!

Thursday 17 December

n a complete panic! And very hungry, because I've got no money and no food!

Saturday 19 December

Yay!

I found my diary!

I was round the back of the hospital, where the kitchens are, hoping that one of the staff might slip me a mug of soup, when I saw it poking out of a wheelie bin.

Whoever stole it from me must have thrown it away, and it ended up here!

I looked to see if my money and phone were there too, but the thief must have kept them.

It's so good to be able to share my thoughts again . . .

The truth is, I'm massively stressed.

I've had no luck getting hold of Holly. Every now and then I try and sneak a call from hotel reception when they're not looking, but she always seems too busy to answer when I do. I've emailed her to ask her to send us some money too, but nothing's come yet. I'm sure everything's fine and they're just hard at work, but it's only five days until Christmas Eve, and at this rate, Father Christmas won't be home in time to deliver the presents!

Monday 21 December

More bad news.

They've got wise to me sleeping in reception, and this morning, they kicked me out. I spent the day walking around Malé, and I ended up in that crowded area that I saw from the ambulance.

How am I going to get Father Christmas out now?

At least the rough sleepers are friendly. They've introduced me to a nice man called Donald, who's given me his cardboard box to sleep in. Somehow I always seem to land on my feet.

Donald even looks a bit like Father Christmas, which makes me feel even more at home. He's human, so he's a little bit taller, but he's got the same kindly blue eyes and big white beard.

He used to be a chef at one of the big hotels in Malé, but it burned down, so he lost his job and ended up on the streets. We spent the evening talking about the Christmases he and his brothers and sisters spent growing up in a place called Kilmarnock. There was always snow on Christmas Day, he said, and although his family didn't have much money, they always hung the house with decorations. One year, Father Christmas brought him a red play kitchen, with little wooden pots and pans, and he thinks that might be what got him into cooking.

When I told him I was a Christmas Elf, he didn't bat an eyelid.

'You'll fit in here, right enough,' he said. 'Back in the day, when it was Christmas at the hotel, I used to dress up and hand out presents to the kiddies. Christmas Elves are ten a penny to me.'

Anyway, I'd better try and sleep, because Donald says the police come round really early in the morning and wake everyone up . . .

The trouble is, as soon as I close my eyes, all I can think about is what a mess I've made of everything.

Tuesday 22 December

I just woke up with the most brilliant idea! I've thought of a way to get Father Christmas out of hospital!

Wednesday 23 December

We're back at the North Pole!

So much has happened, I don't know where to begin!

I guess the best place would be just after I told Donald my plan for how to save Father Christmas.

There was a long pause, while he stroked his white

beard. Then fixing me with his bright blue eyes, he said:

'I'm in!'

The next thing I knew, we were crashing in through the hospital doors and heading for the reception desk. I was wearing a baseball cap and sunglasses, in case anyone recognised me.

'Excuse me,' I said urgently. 'My grandad is . . .' I paused, trying to think of the right word.

'Unwell. He thinks he's—' I wracked my brain. 'A ballerina!'

Obligingly, Donald began to twirl.

The receptionist kept watching, expressionless, so Donald stood on tiptoe, arching his arms above his head so that his fingers touched.

To my eyes, it looked pretty impressive, but there was still no reaction from the receptionist, so Donald took a little run-up, then jumped in the air, stretching out both his legs. Unfortunately, when he landed, his right foot got caught in a wastepaper basket, and he skidded forward, colliding with a large freestanding shelf unit decorated with potted plants.

There was a deafening crash, and everyone in reception – doctors, nurses, porters and patients alike – turned to stare.

The receptionist waited patiently until the last piece of crockery had rocked itself to a standstill.

'Psych ward, third floor,' he said warmly. 'I'll request emergency admission.'

Without delay, Donald and I jumped in the lift.

There was a security door at the entrance to the ward, so we waited for someone to leave so that we could sneak in. Right on cue, out came a crowd of doctors, excitedly discussing Father Christmas's case.

'It's puzzling that there's no sign of trauma on the scans,' said one, as they walked to the open lift.

'Maybe the delusion isn't related to the head injury after all,' suggested another.

'He's below the fifth percentile for height and weight,' said a third. 'Could this be a nutrition issue?'

'I just hope we can find a way to help him,' said a fourth.

'I know,' said a fifth as the lift doors closed. 'It's hard to watch a person suffer like this.'

Just in time, I wedged my foot in the security

door, and Donald and I snuck inside. Quiet as mice, we crept through the ward until we found Father Christmas's room.

'Sugarplum fairies!' exclaimed Father Christmas, looking up from his breakfast tray in alarm. 'Who are you? Get out or I'll call secur—'

'It's me!' I exclaimed, cutting him off. 'I've come to get you out of here.'

'Tog!' he cried. 'Come here, you champion elf!'

He gave me a warm hug, and I quickly explained that Donald had offered to take his place.

'Thank you, Donald,' said Father Christmas, shaking him by the hand. 'I won't forget this.'

Donald was rooted to the spot, his eyes like saucers.

'It's you, isn't it?' he squeaked. 'It's *really* you.'

'How's that little red kitchen set working out for you?' asked Father Christmas, with a twinkle in his eye.

'Father Christmas!' Donald blurted, flinging his arms around his hero. Tears glistened in his eyes as he held on tight, beaming with gratitude.

But there was no time to spare, so I cleared my throat, dropping the hint that we needed to hurry up.

Moments later, Father Christmas was dressed in Donald's old tracksuit, and Donald was tucked up in bed in Father Christmas's hospital gown.

'Ahhh, a bed! What luxury!' said Donald as Father Christmas and I headed for the door. 'This is the best present I've had in years. Thank you, Father Christmas! Thank you, Tog! And good luck!'

Donald's good wishes must have worked, because when we arrived at Malé airport, a plane was just about to leave for Lapland.

This time, I slept all the way, partly because I was really tired after my night in the cardboard box, but also because I was so relieved that Father Christmas was returning home safe and sound, just in time for Christmas!

It was evening when we arrived in Lapland, and the airport car park was caked in snow. Father Christmas gave an elaborate finger whistle, and moments later, Rudolph and the other reindeer came prancing over the horizon, pulling the sleigh!

'Father Christmas!' called Rudolph, as we clambered aboard. 'Are we glad to see you!'

'True dat!' replied Father Christmas, tucking a warm blanket over our knees. I couldn't help but smile, thinking he must have picked that expression up from In-Cent.

Father Christmas shook the reins, and Rudolph and his team bolted forward, pulling the sleigh with a jolt that made me grip the sides tightly. We raced through the airport car park, then suddenly the sleigh leaped into the air, soaring up towards the stars! My stomach dropped with excitement as we climbed higher and higher, the lights of the airport falling away behind us, and the wild wind whistling at our cheeks!

Soon we were leaving the twinkling lights of the airport behind, and sailing over an immense dark forest.

I was beginning to feel that special Christmas feeling, where everything seems brighter, happier, and more magical than ever! Tomorrow was Christmas Eve, and the day after that it would be Christmas!

'It's beautiful!' I called to Father Christmas.

'You haven't seen the tundra yet!' he exclaimed.

Sure enough, snow-covered mountains and frozen lakes opened out in front of us, stretching as far as the eye could see; then, as we approached the coast, we glimpsed the vast Arctic Ocean, littered with icebergs.

'Look!' called Father Christmas, gripping my arm and pointing at something below us.

Below us was a polar bear, lumbering across the ice!

Seeing the bear coming, a group of seals slithered off an

iceberg and vanished in the water.

'*You're not going to catch us this time, Mr Bear!*' Father Christmas grinned, speaking in his mock-seal voice.

I beamed.

'Over there!' Father Christmas exclaimed, pointing again.

It was an enormous grey walrus! As I watched, it used its impressive tusks to haul its rubbery body out of the water, and up on to the ice.

Suddenly I spotted what must have been a dozen more, bobbing in the ocean!

'Merry Christmas!' I called, and Father Christmas laughed.

Then, as we flew further north still, the

temperature plummeted, and the landscape became more and more barren. The animals vanished, and the dark patches of water became fewer and fewer, until all we could see was a vast expanse of snow, shimmering in the moonlight.

It felt like we were far from any living thing, and I felt a pang of loneliness . . .

Then the next thing I knew, we were cresting the uppermost ridge of the Arctic Hills, and the glittering lights of the village rose up to meet us!

It looked miraculous!

I felt a jolt of excitement in my stomach. It had been two long months since I had seen the lights of my hometown, and the thought of being with my family and friends for Christmas was almost too much to bear.

As we flew low over the houses, I could see the warm glow of candles and lanterns shining in the windows, the doors and windowsills hung with decorations, and the roofs dripping with coloured lights. Everyone was getting ready for Christmas! Straining my eyes in the direction of the East Village, I thought for a moment I glimpsed my very own house!

Father Christmas guided the reindeer, and we swooped downwards, skimming the brightly coloured canopies of the market stalls, bustling with shoppers, bystanders and street performers. The air rang with the sound of music and laughter, and the sweet scent of cinnamon, gingerbread and hot cocoa curled in my nostrils.

Finally we looped up and round, heading for

Father Christmas guided the reindeer, and we swooped downwards

Christmas Place, and flew over the ice rink! The Workshop must have closed for the night, because elves of every age, size and shape were out skating in the torchlight. From up in the sleigh, their looping skate tracks looked impossibly beautiful, like lace woven into the ice. To my surprise, at the edge of the rink, I spotted two familiar figures . . .

It was Holly and Ana, building a snowman!

Holly giggled and whispered something in Ana's ear.

An awful thought struck me.

Had Holly told Ana where Father Christmas was hiding?

Was that how the baddies had found us?

Could Ana be one of their spies?

'Hold tight!' called Rudolph, leading us downwards. 'The cobbles can be a little bit bumpy!'

We were coming down to land in Christmas Place!

But there was no need to worry. Rudolph and his team came in at just the right angle, and I barely felt a thing.

'Woah!' called Father Christmas, pulling back on the reins, and the sleigh bumped to a halt in the middle of the courtyard, the reindeer's hoofs clopping to a standstill on the cobbles.

'Made it,' said Father Christmas. 'Just in time.'

I smiled.

'Good work, Tog,' said Father Christmas, putting a hand on my shoulder.

'Just doing my duty, sir,' I replied.

'Speaking of duty,' said Father Christmas, his eyes sparkling in the moonlight. 'How would you and Holly like to join the Sleigh Team? As a token of my gratitude, for keeping me safe this Christmas?'

For a moment, it felt like the world had stopped.

Joining the Sleigh Team is one of the highest honours a Christmas Elf can be given. It means you help load the sleigh with all the presents. I'd never dreamed of reaching such giddy heights!

'You don't have to give me your answer now,' said Father Christmas, misinterpreting my silence.

'Are you kidding?' I exclaimed. 'That's beyond my wildest dreams!'

'I'll take that as a yes, then, shall I?' Father Christmas chuckled.

I couldn't wait to tell Holly, so as soon as Father Christmas and I had said our goodbyes as he went off to inspect the toys being packed in their sacks, I ran as fast as I could to the ice rink. Then, once I spotted her, I ran as slow as I could, because she was still with Ana . . .

The two of them were hurling snowballs at one another, laughing and giggling,.

'Holly!' I called.

Holly's mouth fell open in a mixture of surprise and delight!

'Tog!'

She rushed towards me, and gave me a massive hug.

'You made it! I've been so worried about you. Is Dad okay?'

'Heading home as we speak,' I replied.

'Why didn't you answer my calls?' she asked indignantly.

I explained about my phone, and she soon forgave me.

'I can't believe you're back!' she squealed, hugging me again. 'I missed you so much!'

Over her shoulder, I spotted Ana, watching us.

'There's something you need to know,' I said to Holly.

Holly looked at me with a puzzled smile.

'Ola put your Dad in hospital.'

Holly went white.

'What?'

'He's fine now,' I reassured her. 'Better than ever, in fact. But it was a close-run thing. Someone . . .' I glanced at Ana. 'Told the baddies where we were.'

Holly followed my gaze, and shot me a quizzical look.

'You're not suggesting . . . ?' she asked.

I shrugged, and said simply: 'Did you tell Ana where we were?'

Holly's expression darkened. 'Yes,' she said, 'But Ana's my best friend. She'd never betray us? Would you, Ana?'

Ana gave a little laugh, and shook her head. 'Of course not!' she said.

I began to wonder whether I had made a mistake.

'Tog,' said Holly, 'I think you owe Ana an apology.'

'Sorry, Ana,' I said, uncertainly.

'There,' said Holly. 'I think you two should give each other a hug.'

And that's exactly what we did.

'I got a bit carried away,' I said bravely, giving Ana the warmest smile I could manage. 'Forgive me. Happy Christmas. Are you still working in the reindeer stables?'

Ana nodded.

'Then we're going to be seeing a lot of one another,

because Holly and I –' I paused for dramatic effect – 'have been asked to join the Sleigh Team!'

'WHAT?' shrieked Holly. Then she squealed, drumming her feet up and down in a happy dance!

'THAT'S ALL I'VE EVER WANTED!' she shouted, pulling Ana and me together in a hug. 'Now let's get to bed! You know what tomorrow is?'

'Christmas Eve!' I grinned.

'We did it!' declared Holly, hugging me again. 'We saved Christmas!'

'Almost!' I said. 'Those baddies are still out there, remember?'

Over her shoulder, I spotted Ana, watching us. Was I mistaken, or was there sadness in her eyes?

I guess she's worried that she and Holly won't be hanging out so much, now that I'm back.

Thursday 24 December

YOU ARE NOT GOING TO BELIEVE WHAT HAPPENED TODAY!

I'm going to try and tell you everything, exactly as it unfolded, moment by moment.

I won't give away the ending, but I can tell you this:

If, like me, you thought Christmas was safe this year, you couldn't have been more wrong . . .

I woke up really early, before any of my brothers and sisters. We'd all been up late the night before, catching up on all the news we'd missed, so I knew they'd be sleeping soundly.

As quietly as I could, I dressed in my brand-new Sleigh Team outfit, holding the bells on my boots so they didn't jingle and wake everyone up. Workshop Elves, as you probably know, wear green tunics, but the Sleigh Team wears red, just like Father Christmas!

I couldn't resist admiring myself in the bathroom mirror.

'Hi,' I said to my reflection, in a smooth voice. 'I'm Tog. I work on the Sleigh Team.'

Unfortunately, as I twirled to get a better view of my outfit, I slipped on a small puddle of water, flailing backwards so that my bottom got wedged in the open toilet.

Plum, my youngest sister, burst in, looking sleepy and confused.

'What's going on?' she asked.

I tried to act like nothing had happened, but when I got up, I slipped again, knocking a wastepaper basket full of tissues up into the air.

Plum started laughing, and so did I.

Sometimes, it's best not to take yourself too seriously.

I tucked Plum back into bed, then tiptoed downstairs and out into the street.

The snow outside had frozen in the night, and I went skidding and sliding down the lane, fizzing with excitement about the day ahead. For the first time in our careers, Holly and I would be helping to get Father Christmas's sleigh ready, and there was lots to do!

I arrived at Christmas Place just as Barrow, the Loadmaster Elf, called us all to attention.

'Health and Safety,' he announced, examining all our faces suspiciously, as if one of us had stolen it and he wanted it back.

Holly sidled up to me, and we gave each other a little excited grin.

'What's this?' Barrow asked us all, pointing to the empty sleigh.

I raised my hand.

'New elf,' he said, indicating that I should speak.

'Father Christmas's sleigh,' I said confidently.

'No,' said Barrow self-importantly. 'Absolutely not. This, my colleagues, is not a sleigh. What you see here is seven-point-five tonnes of killing projectile.'

He went on to explain how dangerous it would be if the sleigh crashed, and all the jobs we would have to do to make sure it was safe enough for Father Christmas to ride.

'First, we will inspect the equipment,' he explained. 'Broken harnesses, frayed reins or cracked runners can be hazardous.'

We all nodded in agreement.

'Second, we will refresh the sleigh's decoration,

ensuring Father Christmas has comfy cushions to sit on. He's going on a long journey, and bottom ache can be a real problem.'

Holy and I nodded seriously.

'Third, we will check the weight of each present,' he continued. 'Ensuring that the sleigh isn't overloaded, which could cause it to become unbalanced and potentially dangerous to operate.'

We nodded again.

'Fourth, we will load the presents on to the sleigh. All presents must be securely stowed within Father Christmas's sack. We don't want any presents lost or damaged during the journey, thank you very much. Or, worse, falling from the sleigh and causing injury. Father Christmas cruises at an altitude of up to ten thousand feet, and even so much as a satsuma falling from that height could cause serious concussion.'

Somewhere among us, an elf giggled, and Barrow's face clouded.

The giggling immediately stopped.

'Did I say something funny?' he asked, his voice sharp. 'Perhaps we should just toss everything in willy-nilly and hope for the best?'

There was an awkward pause.

'We are responsible for delivering millions of presents to children all over the world. The safety of them, their parents, grandparents and carers, as well as Father Christmas himself, not to mention the reindeer, is in our hands.'

There were murmurings of agreement.

Barrow cleared his throat and returned to his clipboard.

'And speaking of the reindeer: finally, we will make sure the reindeer are well rested and properly fed with magic oats to ensure that they are in good health and capable of safely pulling the sleigh. Are there any questions?'

After Barrow had answered a number of queries, such as the average weight of a present, and whether snowflakes might make a good decoration for the side of the sleigh, we all set about our tasks. Every hour, Barrow blew a whistle so we could keep track of time, and the day flew past faster than a pack of racing huskies. By the time he blew his final whistle, we were all exhausted.

The sleigh looked magnificent! Its sides had been freshly painted in green, and decorated with shiny silver snowflakes; the red velvet seats were fluffed and cosy; the harness and reins were gleaming in the lamplight; and the delivery sack, bulging with presents, was fastened securely on the back.

The sleigh looked magnificent!

It was now very nearly six o'clock, the time when Father Christmas sets off. Holly and I lined up alongside our fellow Sleigh Elves, ready for Barrow's inspection, and I glanced up, breathing in deeply, trying to etch the moment in my memory. The crisp night sky was littered with stars, twinkling like diamonds, casting the entire courtyard in a soft, silvery glow.

'Holly, Tog,' called Barrow, and we snapped to attention.

'Yes, Mister Loadmaster, sir!' we said in unison.

'Good work today. Would you kindly do me the honour of fetching the reindeer?'

Holly and I looked at each other in delight, and ran to the stables. The reindeer were all brushed and ready to go, but there was no sign of Ana.

We heard the sound of sobbing coming from

155

behind the feed hoppers, and behind them, we found Ana, head in hands, crying.

'What's wrong?' asked Holly, kneeling down beside her and putting her arm around Ana's shoulders.

Ana wiped her eyes with the back of her sleeve.

'Nothing,' said Ana, swallowing hard. 'I'm just a bit homesick, that's all.'

'Homesick?' I asked.

'She grew up in Luxembourg,' explained Holly, glancing up at me. 'Her family are Woodland Elves. She's missing them really badly.'

'Oh I see,' I replied. Eva Klutch, the leader of the baddies, was from Luxembourg, and I was about to ask Ana whether she knew her, when Holly cut me off.

'Don't worry, Ana,' she said kindly. 'Christmas is nearly over. You'll see them really soon.'

Ana did her best to smile.

'Now, have you given the reindeer their magic oats?' Holly asked gently. 'It's time to harness them up.'

Ana nodded. Then she burst into tears again, and ran off.

'Best to leave her,' said Holly. 'The pressure gets to everyone. I'm feeling it myself, to be honest. Come on – we need to get these guys harnessed up before Dad arrives.'

As we led the reindeer into the courtyard, the gates to Christmas Place flew open and crowds of people poured in from the village, chattering and laughing with excitement, swarming around the sleigh, warm torchlight flickering on their faces. As Holly and I walked the reindeer into place at the front of the sleigh, I felt a jolt of pride.

'Good luck,' I whispered, placing the harness on Rudolph's back.

'Want me to put in a good word?' murmured my old friend under his breath.

'What do you mean?' I asked, fastening his breastplate.

'There are two seats on the sleigh,' said the reindeer, out of the corner of his mouth. 'Wanna ride shotgun?'

I looked at Holly, who was adjusting the breeching straps.

'If he's offering you a ride,' she said, 'I'd take it.'

'You don't mind?' I asked.

Holly grinned. 'You've earned it,' she said.

A cheer went up from the crowd, and we turned to see Father Christmas marching down the steps of Christmas Lodge, dressed in his finest red velvet.

'Ho ho ho!' he called, waving in delight as the crowd surged forward.

'Back, everyone – back!' called Barrow, clearing a path for the sleigh to pass through. The reindeer began to paw the ground restlessly, the bells on their harnesses jingling merrily.

Father Christmas exchanged a few words with Rudolph, then hoisted himself up into the sleigh, his rosy cheeks glowing in the dancing shadows of the elves' torches.

'Tog,' he said, with a broad grin. 'Would you like to join?

Another cheer went up, as he pulled me up beside him.

'Are you sure?' I said, cupping my hand around his ear, so that he could hear me above the excited hubbub. 'You can change your mind if you want to.'

'Of course I am!' He chuckled in mock outrage.

'If it wasn't for you, I wouldn't be feeling nearly so fresh and Christmas-ready.' He winked. 'I'm ready for anything. That holiday of ours has done me a power of good.'

'Sorry to interrupt, sir!' called Barrow from the crowd. 'But it's six o'clock!'

'Yah!' called Santa, giving the reins a shake, and Rudolph and his team leaned forward, straining under the weight of the sleigh. Barrow was right! It weighed a tonne. Or seven-point-five tonnes, to be precise.

For an awful moment, it seemed like the load was too great, with Dancer losing her footing and almost taking a tumble!

But our hard work paid off, and the harness held her in place.

A group of elves rushed forward to help, and with Dancer back on her feet, Rudolph and his team pulled hard once again. Suddenly the sleigh broke free of the ice that had formed around the rails, and we were gliding over the snow!

I felt a surge of happiness and excitement, and it was as much as I could do to stay in my seat!

If only I'd known what was going to happen next . . .

I'll never tire of riding in the sleigh!

After take-off, Rudolph led us over the entire village. Everywhere I looked, there were elves cheering us on: stallholders waving from the market place; skaters calling from the ice rink. Every street, doorway and window was crowded with elves sending their good wishes.

Finally, we swooped over Christmas Lodge, Father Christmas's home at the foot of the Arctic Hills, where Gerda, his wife, was the last to wave us off.

Then, the reindeer began to climb, and we crested a steep ridge, leaving the twinkling lights of the village behind. The snowfields of the Arctic lay ahead of us, and a bright moon rose slowly to our left, casting eerie shadows across the snow. Icebergs gave way to dark ocean, and soon the coast of Norway appeared on the horizon, its towns and cities glowing in the distance like glittering spider webs.

'Who's our first delivery for?' I shouted, buffeted by the wind.

'A little girl called Ingrid Olsen, in Tromsø,' answered Father Christmas. 'She wants a kit for making her own jewellery. Check the delivery sack — it should be close to hand.'

But as I turned, the sleigh suddenly started to drop! We were losing altitude!

'Whoa!' I cried, as my stomach lurched.

'What's happening, Rudolph?' called Father Christmas.

'I don't know!' called Rudolph, as he and the other reindeer struggled to keep the sleigh in the air.

'Did you have your magic oats?' called Father Christmas.

'Yes!' replied Rudolph in exasperation. 'Though . . .' He paused, as if remembering something. 'They did taste a bit funny.'

I screwed my face up in confusion.

'I don't understand,' I said. 'The stable-boy has been sacked and sent to Cloudberry Prison. So how could he have done this?'

'It's beyond me,' said Father Christmas.

And then an awful thought struck me.

Ana had been helping out with the reindeer. And she was being a bit odd . . . What if I was right, and she was working with the baddies? But then why she was crying?

'Look out!' called Rudolph, as we began to plummet downwards!

'We're going to have to make an emergency landing!' yelled Father Christmas.

'Where?' called Rudolph.

A group of islands was coming up fast, but they all appeared to be rocky with nowhere to land. Then suddenly I spotted something!

'There!' I called above the rushing wind. 'A beach!'

'Got it!' called Rudolph. He and his team were

'Look out!' called Rudolph

now galloping at full stretch, doing their best to level out the sleigh.

'Hold on tight!' he called, and Father Christmas and I gripped the sides of the sleigh, our knuckles turning white.

There was a strange pause when everything went quiet, and we seemed to be floating in a different time and place . . .

BANG!

We landed with a bump on white sand, the reindeer's hoofs pounding ahead of us, the ocean flashing past on one side, and craggy rocks on the other!

'Woah!' called Father Christmas, pulling back on the reins. 'Woah!'

'Oh my goodness,' panted Rudolph, and we slid to a halt, dark waves crashing beside us. 'We've lost a runner, look!'

It was true: a freshly-painted wooden plank lay on the sand beside us.

Father Christmas and I exchanged concerned glances. We were on a tiny island, surrounded by water! How would we get off? And, even more importantly, how would we deliver the presents?

I opened my mouth to speak, but before I could form my words, a mechanical growl cut through the darkness, building to a roar!

It was the sound of a motorboat, powering towards us!

Our hearts sank as we saw Eva in the cockpit, surrounded by Ola, Max and Fizz.

The baddies had caught us!

'Well, well, well!' cackled Eva as her boat pulled alongside the stranded sleigh. 'If it isn't Father Christmas himself! We meet again.'

'What are you doing here?' asked Father Christmas sternly.

'What does it look like?' replied Eva. 'We're here to take those presents and sell them off to the highest bidder!'

'You'll never get away with it,' I warned. 'None of your other stupid plans have worked – the teddy bear, the ice skates, the *hospital*.'

'Oh, but we will!' Ola grinned, stepping ashore. 'True, there were a few hiccups. But we've been planning this grand finale for weeks. Thanks to your little emergency landing, we've got you right where we want you.'

'Not for long,' muttered Father Christmas, scanning the dark horizon as though searching for any sign of help.

'If you're looking for Holly,' said Eva cruelly,

'she's not coming. My daughter Ana is keeping an eye on her.'

I gasped in shock.

Ana was Eva's daughter!

I was right – Ana was a baddy!

'Now, hand over those presents,' demanded Eva, brandishing a pair of old-fashioned Luxembourgian muskets, and pointing them right at me and Father Christmas. 'And no funny business.'

'We can't do that,' said Father Christmas firmly. 'Those presents are meant for the children of the world.'

Max and Fizz were grinning from ear to ear, clearly eager to join the heist. As Father Christmas and I watched helplessly, they splashed through the surf, joining with Ola in loading the sack of presents on to the boat.

'Farewell, suckers!' called Eva, and with an evil laugh, she opened up the throttle, the boat powering away across the dark water, kicking up a deluge of spray that left Father Christmas and me drenched to the bone.

But Father Christmas wasn't giving up that easily.

As many people know, Christmas Elves can work at super-human speed; that's how we get all the toys made before the big day. In a surge of wild, righteous energy, Father Christmas snatched up the reins, twirling them around his head like a lasso, before flinging them out across the ocean!

He leaped aboard the runner, and took off across the sand, waterskiing behind Eva's motorboat! Then, as Eva tried to make a turn, he skied past her, firing water in all directions, and disabling her engine as he passed! His arc of travel brought him neatly back up on the sand, and he began to haul the boat towards him, reeling the presents in like a prize catch!

'Bravo,' said Eva, sarcastically, as the boat bumped up against the shore. 'Now we're all stranded!'

My shoulders slumped as I realised she was right. We had the presents, but without a working sleigh, there was no way we could deliver them.

A feeling of hopelessness washed over me, turning rapidly to despair, as I heard the whirring of rotor blades, and looked up to see a helicopter, marked with Eva's family crest, and piloted by Ana!

I knew exactly what was going to happen next.

Ana would rescue the baddies, and take the presents!

But I was wrong!

Instead, a second figure moved within the helicopter, opening the side door and throwing something out. My mouth fell open in surprise. It was Holly!

WHUMP!

A sack landed on the sand beside us, and out spilled . . .

Magic oats!

'I'm sorry, Mum,' said Ana, speaking over the loudhailer, her voice echoing all around us. As she spoke, a searchlight trapped us all in its glare.

'I can't do it! I don't want to let my new friends down. I don't want to ruin Christmas, or be on the Naughty List any more — I want to have a normal Christmas, with presents under the tree, like all the other kids!'

'Stupid girl!' howled Eva. 'I wanted those things too, but I never got them, so why should you?'

It was then that Father Christmas turned to me

and in a quiet voice, so that only I could hear, said:

'Is she crying?'

Now he mentioned it, I could see he was right: Eva Klutch, the notorious villain, had tears in her eyes.

'And anyway,' said Eva, grimacing with the effort of pushing her feelings back down, 'it's too late. You think they'll still be your friends after this?'

'Actually,' said Father Christmas, 'I've always been a firm believer in second chances.'

Eva eyed him suspiciously.

'How would you and Ana like to spend Christmas with me, at Christmas Lodge?'

Eva's eyes welled with tears, and for the first time since I'd known her – and quite possibly, her whole life – she smiled, nodding gratefully, and I saw the little girl inside her, basking in the glow of warmth and kindness that was Father Christmas.

'What about Ola?' she asked. 'Can he come too?'

'Of course!' roared Father Christmas. 'And Max, and Fizz. To host you all would be my pleasure.'

But as we'd been talking, Ola had found some oars in the boat, and was busy rowing away, making his getaway with Max and Fizz.

'Never!' he called, as the three of them vanished into the dark.

Was it me, or did Max and Fizz look a little sad?

But there was no time to waste. Grabbing the bag of magic oats, I fed the reindeer, making sure each one in turn had plenty of fuel for the long journey ahead. Then Father Christmas and I jumped back on the sleigh, the reindeer circling round in the sand, then powering along the beach, before leaping into the air, leading us off towards the lights of Tromsø.

As I looked back, I saw Holly drop a ladder from

the helicopter so that Eva could climb up.

I smiled to myself.

Father Christmas is right: everyone deserves a second chance.

Christmas Day

Today's celebration lunch at Christmas Lodge was incredible!

A roaring fire crackled in the fireplace, and candles flickered on all the tables, lighting our smiling faces. The walls shimmered with evergreen garlands, and twinkling fairy lights danced across the ceiling.

Holly and I sat side by side, laughing and chatting, while Eva and Ana had the honour of sitting at the head of the table with Father Christmas. The entire Workshop congratulated one another on another successful Christmas, and Nutmeg – who has been cleared of all charges – was even voted Elf of the Year, receiving a thunderous round of applause.

After the feast, Father Christmas and I stepped outside into the cool, crisp air.

'This is perfect,' I said, admiring the peaceful Arctic Hills.

'Almost,' replied Father Christmas, wearing a sly grin.

I looked at him curiously.

He leaned in and whispered, 'I'm going to make an important change.'

'What's that?' I asked, intrigued.

'I'm giving everyone a holiday.'

And as if the entire North Pole agreed with him, at that moment, the sky lit up with the northern lights, painting ribbons of colour across the sky.

CONTINUE THE
CHRISTMAS MAGIC

'A sheer delight for kids both big and Small'
Ruth Jones, Award-winning writer and comedian

The
Night I Met
Father
Christmas

The bestselling author actor and comedian

BEN MILLER

Chapter One

When I was small, one of my friends said something really silly. He said that Father Christmas didn't exist.

'So where do all the Christmas presents come from?' I asked him. He didn't have an answer.

'I don't know,' he said. 'It's just something my older sister told me.'

'Who comes down the chimney and eats the mince pies and drinks the brandy?' I asked. 'Who rides the sleigh?'

My friend was silent for a while.

'You know what?' he said. 'You're right. I don't know why I brought it up. Do you want to play marbles?'

That night, I had trouble getting to sleep. I had won the argument, but my friend had planted a tiny seed of doubt in my mind. What if Father Christmas *wasn't* real?

As Christmas approached, I began to ask myself all sorts of worrying questions: who *was* Father Christmas? Why did he bring presents? How did he deliver them all in one night? How did it all start?

I made up my mind that there was only one way to find out the truth. I had to meet Father Christmas, face to face.

Of course, I didn't tell anyone about my plan. My parents would have tried to stop me, and my twin sisters would have wanted to tag along, even though they were much too young. This was a serious operation and I couldn't risk it going wrong.

Finally, Christmas Eve arrived, and my parents came up to kiss me goodnight.

'Do you know what day it is tomorrow?' asked my mother, her eyes twinkling.

'Is it Wednesday?' I asked, pretending not to care.

She looked at my father, who shrugged.

'Yes, darling,' she said, trying to maintain an air of suspense. 'It is Wednesday. But it's also Christmas Day.'

'Oh,' I said. 'I'm not really that interested in Christmas.'

'Really?' said my father. They both looked very disappointed, and for a very brief moment I felt bad for tricking them.

'It's okay, I suppose,' I said, 'if you like presents and chocolate and sweets and things like that, but I prefer to work through a few maths problems while listening to classical music.' And then I faked a big yawn and closed my eyes.

'Whatever makes you happy, darling,' said my mother, sounding worried. They kissed me goodnight, switched out the light, and went downstairs.

I lay there in the dark, with my eyes closed, listening. I could hear my sisters in their bedroom down the hall, talking in their own special made-up language, which only they could understand. Usually, when I heard them talking like that it made me feel a bit left out, but not tonight, because I knew that I was doing something very special.

Eventually, my sisters fell quiet and the house suddenly seemed very deep and dark. I could hear the low murmur of my parents talking downstairs, but soon that stopped too, and then the stairs creaked as they made their way up to bed.

I knew they might look in on me, so I acted as if I was fast asleep.

'Goodnight, little man,' my father whispered, as he gently moved my head back on to the pillow and pulled the covers up to keep me warm. Then I smelled my mother's perfume as she gave me a kiss. The door closed, and I heard their footsteps crossing the landing to their bedroom.

I lay still, listening in the darkness. After what felt like the longest time, I decided it was safe enough to half-open one eye. My bedside clock showed a quarter to twelve. I had never, ever been awake that late before, and I wondered for a moment if, when it struck midnight, I would be turned to stone, like a child in a fairy tale.

I pulled back the covers, swung my feet

down on to the rug and tiptoed to the window. Outside, the window ledge was covered in snow. The moon was thin but bright, and in our neighbour's garden a fox picked its way across the white lawn. Above me, the blue-black sky was scattered with stars and little wisps of cloud. Nothing moved. No shooting stars, no satellites, not even a trundling planet. And definitely no reindeer-drawn sleigh.

I slunk back into bed. Using both pillows, together with one of the cushions from the chair, I made a sort of bed-throne, so that I could sit up and watch the open sky. Whatever happened, I wasn't going to sleep. I was going to wait until Father Christmas came.

BEN MILLER is an actor, comedian, director, and the bestselling author of magical stories for all the family:

The Night I Met Father Christmas,
The Boy Who Made the World Disappear,
The Day I Fell Into a Fairytale,
How I Became a Dog Called Midnight,
The Night We Got Stuck in a Story,
Diary of a Christmas Elf,
Secrets of a Christmas Elf.

@actualbenmiller

TURN THE PAGE, SHARE THE ADVENTURE WITH BEN MILLER